For Nick

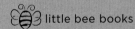 little bee books

An imprint of Bonnier Publishing Group
853 Broadway, New York, New York 10003
Copyright © 2016 by Jo Williamson
First published in Great Britain by Scholastic.
This little bee books edition, 2016.
All rights reserved, including the right of
reproduction in whole or in part in any form.
LITTLE BEE BOOKS is a trademark of Bonnier Publishing Group,
and associated colophon is a trademark of Bonnier Publishing Group.
Manufactured in Johor Bahru, Malaysia 62973
First Edition 10 9 8 7 6 5 4 3 2 1
Library of Congress Cataloging-in-Publication Data is available upon request.
ISBN 978-1-4998-0266-5
littlebeebooks.com
bonnierpublishing.com

Molly starts each day looking lovely and clean . . .

Molly's
dog Pip

. . . but it never ever lasts.

This week, Molly decides to practice staying neat and tidy
because she is singing in the school show on Saturday . . .
in a lovely new white dress.

On Monday, it rained.

Luckily, I have my umbrella.

The rain had stopped on Tuesday . . .

. . . so dodging the puddles on her scooter was a fun way for Molly to get to school.

I'm sure the teacher won't notice a bit of mud.

On Wednesday, Molly tried to bake some cupcakes, wearing her apron to keep her dress spick-and-span.

On Thursday, Mom bought
Molly her favorite ice cream . . .

. . . the TRIPLE double-decker cone
with cherries and a dollop
of raspberry sauce.

Ooh,
triple
trouble!

Molly's only mistake on Friday . . .

. . . was not wearing her GREEN dress.

Come on, Pip.
Let's go home.

And now Saturday was here.
Molly loved her dress . . .

. . . and would try very, VERY hard not to get messy.

Okay, Pip, you can come, but we are not going to the park.

Molly thought it was safer to leave the troublesome
scooter at home and walk to school.

An ice cream would be nice . . . but maybe not today.

She noticed the puddles . . .
just in time.

Molly was almost
at school, but . . .

. . . WATCH OUT!

Phew! That was close.

Molly had made it!

She was SO proud that she had managed to keep her dress clean.

Well . . . ALMOST!